The strange case of
Dr. Jekyll
&
Mr. Hyde

KU-568-996

Adapted by Rob Lloyd Jones

Illustrated by Victor Tavares

Reading consultant: Alison Kelly
Roehampton University

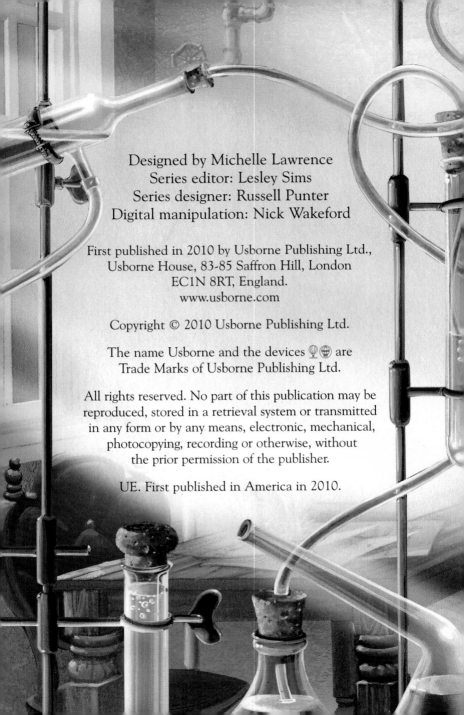

Designed by Michelle Lawrence
Series editor: Lesley Sims
Series designer: Russell Punter
Digital manipulation: Nick Wakeford

First published in 2010 by Usborne Publishing Ltd.,
Usborne House, 83-85 Saffron Hill, London
EC1N 8RT, England.
www.usborne.com

UE. First published in America in 2010.

Contents

Chapter 1

The story of the door

It was a cold night in London. The full moon hung low over the city's rickety rooftops, and wisps of fog floated like ghosts through the squalid streets.

Two men strode side by side along a lamplit lane, their footsteps echoing around the old walls. Their names were Mr. Utterson and Mr. Enfield. They walked together every Sunday, but they rarely spoke.

Until this night.

"You see that door?" Enfield said, prodding his cane towards a dark doorway. "I know a strange story about that door."

Utterson's bushy eyebrows rose in interest. "Go on," he urged.

"It was a drizzly night last month," Enfield continued. "I was just leaving a tavern nearby, when a man came charging over the cobbles, so fast he ran straight into a little girl coming from the other direction. The poor child screamed, but the fellow simply trampled over her and kept running."

"Surely it was an accident?" Utterson said.

"Hardly," Enfield scoffed. "Utterson, the man laughed. I hear it in my head even now – a terrible, high-pitched cackle that sent a shiver down my spine."

"What did you do?" Utterson asked.

"Well, I set off after the man and tackled him. But when I saw his face, I wished I hadn't. His eyes were so dark they were almost black, and his mouth was twisted into a sinister sneer. I swear he looked like the Devil himself."

"Come now Enfield," Utterson laughed. "Surely you exaggerate?"

"I am not sure that I do, Utterson. The very sight of this man made my stomach turn. Still, I composed myself and dragged him back to the scene of his crime. The girl was crying, and her family yelled for the police."

"How did the fellow react to that?"

"The man's face broke into a vicious smile. He told them that he wished to avoid a scene, and offered the family a hundred pounds to remain silent about the incident."

"Did they accept?" Utterson asked.

"They did. The sinister figure led us to this very house, where he produced the money and simply tossed it to the ground. Then he turned and slammed the door in our faces."

Enfield and Utterson continued strolling through the gaslight.

"I tell you Utterson," Enfield said, "never in my life have I met such a fiend. I am still haunted by the memory of his ghoulish face and brutal manner."

Utterson smiled at his friend's dramatic descriptions. "I shall be careful to avoid him," he replied. "Did he give you his name?"

"He did. His name was Edward Hyde."

Utterson's smile disappeared. "Hyde?" he said. "Are you quite sure?"

"Does the name mean something to you?"

"No," Utterson muttered, "it means nothing to me."

But Utterson was lying. The name Edward Hyde haunted him too, but for a very different reason...

Chapter 2

Search for Mr. Hyde

That evening, Utterson sat in his house beside a crackling fire, gazing at a document in his hand. Utterson was a lawyer, and this document was the will he had written for his close friend Dr. Henry Jekyll. Its final line had occupied his thoughts for months, but never more so than tonight...

In the event of my death or disappearance, all of my possessions are to pass into the hands of Mr. Edward Hyde.

Utterson had known Henry for most of his life, but had never heard the name Hyde before he read it in this will. And now here Hyde was again, in Enfield's terrible tale. What hold did such a fiend have over poor Henry?

"If anyone knows," Utterson thought, "it will be Lanyon."

An hour later, he arrived at the house of his friend Hastie Lanyon, a red-faced doctor with slicked silver hair. They sipped wine and spoke happily of old times. He and Lanyon were university friends, where they had both known Henry Jekyll.

"Did Henry ever mention a friend of his to you Lanyon?" Utterson asked. "A man named Edward Hyde?"

"Hyde?" Lanyon said. "No, never heard of him. But I have not spoken to Henry for almost a year. We might both be doctors, but he began to speak such unscientific balderdash that I feared he had lost his mind. Now, let us talk of a happier subject..."

But all Utterson could think of was that sinister name in Henry Jekyll's will. "If he is Mr. Hyde," the lawyer decided, "then I shall be Mr. Seek."

From that night on, Utterson began to haunt the door that Enfield had shown him. Before work in the morning and after work at night, he hid in an alley and waited for a glimpse of the mysterious fiend.

At last, his patience was rewarded. Footsteps echoed along the foggy street. A hunched figure emerged from the gloom.

Utterson stepped out, blocking the man's path. "Mr. Hyde I think?" he said.

The man shrank back with a hissing intake of breath. His face remained hidden under the shadow of his crooked top hat. "How do you know me?" he snapped.

"First," Utterson asked, "will you let me see your face?"

Hyde hesitated, and then stepped closer to the street lamp. Utterson shivered when he saw the man in the light. It was hard to say what was wrong with him, just that there was something evil about his face. A line of spit hung from his mouth as he kept grinding his rotten teeth.

"Now," Hyde snarled. "Tell me how you know me?"

"Henry Jekyll gave me your address."

At this, Hyde broke into a savage laugh. He barged past Utterson, knocking the lawyer to the ground. The door slammed behind him as he disappeared into the house.

Utterson sat on the cobbles, trying to calm his hammering heart. Poor Henry, he thought. What can this devil have over him?

Chapter 3

Visiting Dr. Jekyll

Utterson barely slept that night. The leering face of Edward Hyde haunted his dreams. He saw those burning eyes and that cruel, sneering smile. The bedroom rang with the man's mocking laugh.

The following morning, he took a carriage
to Henry Jekyll's house, a marble-stepped
mansion with flowers hanging by the door.
Inside, the doctor greeted Utterson with a
friendly handshake and beaming smile.

As they ate breakfast together, Utterson
studied his old friend. He was the same age
as Utterson and Lanyon, but always seemed
ten years younger. He certainly didn't look
like a man stalked by a sinister enemy. But
Utterson had to be sure...

"I want to talk about that will of yours,"
he announced over coffee.

Jekyll's smile vanished. "I asked you never to speak of it Utterson," he said.

"And I hoped not to," Utterson told him. "Except I have since heard more about this man Edward Hyde. Henry, what I heard was abominable."

"I am aware that you met him," Jekyll said, "and that he was uncivil to you."

"Uncivil? This man is a fiend Henry. And yet you have left him your entire fortune in your will. Tell me what hold he has over you."

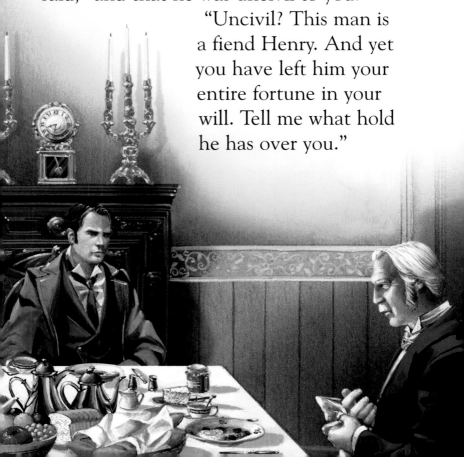

Jekyll rose. The firelight cast his shadow long and monstrous across the wall.

"I cannot tell you," he said. "All I can say is that I fear there will soon come a time when I am no longer here. In that case, promise me you will give everything I own to Edward Hyde. Help me Utterson, if not as my lawyer, then as my friend."

How could Utterson refuse? Picking up his hat and cane, he left the doctor alone. "I can't pretend I shall ever like Hyde," he said as he went. "But I promise."

Chapter 4

An inspector calls

Utterson agreed to let the issue of Hyde drop, but a few months later it thrust itself back into his life in a chilling manner.

It was a blustery Wednesday night when Utterson was woken by a knock on his front door. He lit a candle and carried the flickering light to the entrance. A police inspector stood outside with a grim look on his face.

"Mr. Utterson?" he asked. "I have a dark story to tell you."

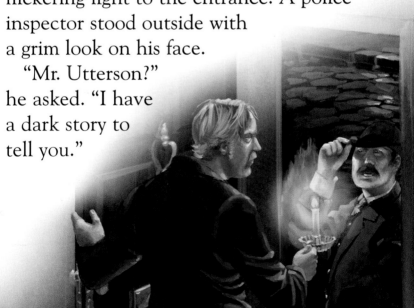

Utterson lit a fire, as the inspector sat down and began his tale.

"It began across London," the inspector said, "as a maidservant looked out of her window before she slept. She saw an elderly gentleman who had lost his way in the night. The maid was about to offer directions, when another fellow came towards him, a man she describes as short and hunched."

A shiver ran down Utterson's spine. "Go on," he said.

"Well," the inspector continued, "all of a sudden this fellow broke into a rage. He struck the old man to the ground, and rained blows upon him with his cane. At the sight of such a terrible thing, the poor maid fainted."

"And the old man?"

"He is dead," the inspector said. "It is murder, Mr. Utterson."

The inspector reached into his coat pocket. He brought out the broken end of a walking cane. "Do you recognize this?" he asked.

Utterson did. It was a cane he gave to Henry Jekyll years ago. Inscribed on the handle was a message:

To Henry, from your friend Gabriel Utterson.

"So you see why I have come to you," the inspector said. "This was the murderer's stick. Who is this man 'Henry'?"

"It is Henry Jekyll."

"Then he is our killer."

"No," Utterson insisted, "Jekyll is a tall man. The maid described someone short. Inspector, I think I know the real name of the murderer. It is Edward Hyde, and I will gladly take you to his house."

The hunt was on. The inspector marched behind Utterson as the first glimmers of daylight lit the empty streets. Soon, they arrived in that dismal district, and at that decrepit door. Hyde's door.

The inspector pounded on it with his fist. "Edward Hyde!" he called. "I demand to speak to you."

No reply. The door creaked open on its rusty hinges. Utterson stepped back, happy to let the inspector lead the way inside.

It was morning outside, but the house was dark and dingy within. Drawers hung open and clothes lay strewn across the floor. Among them, Utterson spotted shirts and jackets belonging to Henry Jekyll. "So Hyde is a thief as well as a murderer," he whispered.

The inspector gestured for him to be quiet, as they crept deeper into the house. A fire crackled in the drawing room, but there was no one home.

"Looks like we have missed our man," Utterson said.

The inspector picked something up from the floor. It was the other half of Hyde's broken walking stick. He raised the evidence triumphantly. "The murder weapon," he declared. "We have Mr. Hyde now."

Chapter 5

The incident of the letter

It was late afternoon by the time Utterson arrived at Henry Jekyll's house. The doctor's butler, Poole, greeted him with a worried frown.

"My master is in sir," he said, "but he is in strange spirits."

Poole led Utterson to a laboratory at the back of the house. Light fell dimly through a crack in the curtains, illuminating a clutter of test tubes, strange potions in jars and powders corked in bottles.

Henry Jekyll sat slumped in an armchair. His eyes were red and his skin had turned deathly pale.

"Have you heard the news about your friend Hyde?" Utterson asked. "The police are searching for him across London."

Jekyll groaned in despair. "Utterson, I swear that I am done with Edward Hyde. Mark my words, that terrible man will never be heard from again. But there is one last thing..."

Jekyll held up a crumpled sheet of paper. The page trembled in his hand. "A messenger brought this letter today from Hyde," he said. "It says that he has run away and will never return. Do with it what you want, old friend."

"And what about your will Henry? Should I remove Hyde's name from that document?"

Jekyll stared up at the dusky light leaking between the curtains. Utterson saw a look of desperate sadness in his friend's eyes.

"No," Jekyll said finally. "Leave the will as it is. Just in case..."

With that, the doctor sank into his chair, covering his face with his hands.

As he left the house, Utterson turned to the butler. "Poole?" he asked. "There was a letter delivered today. Did you see what the messenger looked like?"

Poole looked puzzled. "We have received no letters today sir," he said.

A dark thought entered Utterson's
mind. He took Hyde's letter from
his pocket and folded the bottom to
conceal the sender's name. "Tell me
Poole," he asked, "do you recognize this
handwriting?"

Poole studied the page closely, and then
nodded. "It looks different sir. But I swear
this letter was written by Dr. Jekyll."

Utterson stumbled into the dusky
streets, his mind reeling. Could it be
possible? Could Henry Jekyll be covering
for a murderer?

Chapter 6

A face at the window

Time ran on, and the hunt for Edward Hyde continued all over London. Thousands of pounds were offered in reward. But he had no family, and no photographs had ever been taken of him. Those who had seen his face found that they could not really describe him, other than to agree that he was a detestable-looking man.

As the weeks passed, Utterson thought less of Hyde, and more of Henry, who had become a new man. The doctor invited Utterson and Lanyon for dinner, and the three friends talked and laughed about old times. It was as if a dark cloud had lifted from over him.

Then, two months later, the cloud returned. It was a crisp January evening, and Utterson was on one of his walks through the city. He decided to pay Henry a visit.

But when he reached the doctor's house, Poole wouldn't let him in. "My master is confined to the house today," the butler said.

"Is he sick?" Utterson asked.

"Sir," Poole said, his face darkening, "I cannot say what is wrong with him."

Worried, Utterson marched around to the back of the house. He called to the laboratory window, "Henry! Are you unwell?"

A curtain rustled in the breeze. Moments later, Henry Jekyll appeared at the window. He looked like a prisoner in a dungeon, with pale skin and sunken eyes. "I am very low Utterson," he said drearily.

"You stay indoors too much," Utterson said. "Get your hat and come for a walk."

Jekyll smiled sadly. "You are a good friend Utterson," he said, "but I am afraid we can never meet again. From now on I intend to remain confined to my house."

"My dear chap, whatever for?"

"I have brought upon myself a punishment I cannot name. Ask Lanyon, he will tell you..."

Before Utterson could reply, Jekyll gave a terrific cry. He gritted his teeth and bent over, as if fighting some terrible pain. But the pain was too much.

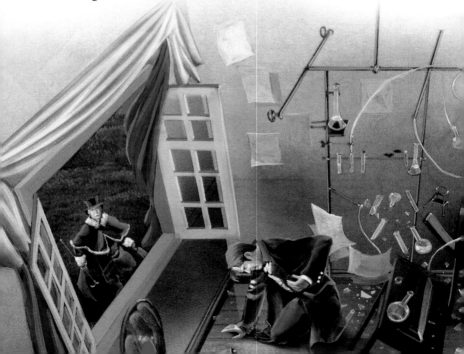

The doctor collapsed back, clutching his stomach and crying out again.

Utterson heard a table crash over, and glass smash. Then, suddenly, the window slammed shut.

"Henry..." Utterson whispered. "What has become of you?"

He rushed to Lanyon's house. But there, too, he found his friend unwell.

Lanyon lay in bed, the blanket pulled up to his chin. Each time a door creaked or a window rattled in the wind, the doctor's eyes darted around the room. It seemed as if the man's nerves had been shattered.

"I have had a shock Utterson," he said in a trembling voice, "from which I fear I shall never recover."

"Henry is ill too," Utterson said. "Have you seen him?"

A terrified whimper escaped Lanyon's lips. He sank deeper under his covers.

"I wish to hear no more of Dr. Jekyll," he said, spitting the name like poison.

"But Lanyon," Utterson protested, "we three are old friends. I fear that Henry needs our help."

Lanyon gave a hollow laugh, which turned into a hacking cough. "Sit down Utterson," he said, "and I will tell you a story about our friend Henry Jekyll, and the help that I have *already* given him."

Utterson drew a chair closer as Hastie Lanyon began his tale...

Chapter 7

Dr. Lanyon's tale

"Four days ago," Lanyon told Utterson, "I was sitting alone at home when a messenger brought a letter. It was from Henry Jekyll."

> Dear Hastie,
>
> I beg you to help me. Upon receipt of this letter, proceed directly to the laboratory in my house. Remove the top drawer from the desk and carry it back to your home. At midnight, a man will come to collect it. Give it to him and ask no questions.
>
> Please Lanyon do as I ask! My life depends upon it.
>
> Your friend, Henry.

"A strange request," Utterson said. "Did you carry it out?"

"How could I not?" Lanyon replied. "I took a carriage straight to Henry's house, where Poole let me into the laboratory. The room was in a terrible state, Utterson.

There were test tubes smashed across the floor, powders and potions spilled over desks, and notebooks scribbled with the results of failed experiments. More and more I feared that Henry Jekyll had lost his mind."

"But you found the drawer he mentioned in his letter?" Utterson asked.

"I did. It contained several jars of powder that looked like salt, but smelled unlike anything I have known. One sniff of the foul chemicals made me dizzy."

"Did you bring the drawer back here, as Henry asked?"

"I wish I had not Utterson. For what happened next has left me a broken man."

"Go on..."

"This was obviously a secret matter," Lanyon said, "so I sent my servants to bed and awaited the arrival of Henry's mysterious visitor. The chimes of midnight had barely struck when there came a fierce knock on my door. A dwarfish figure stood silhouetted in the porch light. He seemed agitated, unable to stand still.

'Have you got it?' the man snarled.

'Won't you come inside first?' I asked."

"The man shuffled into the light. Utterson, he was a repugnant figure. He kept grinding his teeth and muttering furiously to himself."

Utterson pulled his chair even closer to Lanyon's bed. "This man," he said, "sounds like Edward Hyde."

"That was my fear too," replied Lanyon. "I wished then that I had not invited the ghastly individual into my house."

"What did he do next?" Utterson asked.

"He grew angry, Utterson.

'Where is it?' he growled. 'Where is the drawer? Tell me!'

'Compose yourself sir,' I told him. 'The drawer is over there.'

The man sprang at it with ferocious relish. A hideous grin spread across his face as he opened one of the jars of powder. 'Yes,' he said, hissing the word like a snake. 'Now, give me a glass of water,' he demanded."

"You gave it to him?" Utterson asked.

"I am not ashamed to say that I was scared, Utterson. I simply wanted the man gone. So I fetched him the water, and he poured the powder into the glass. The mixture bubbled and frothed. Vile-smelling fumes swirled into the air. Another evil smile spread across the man's face.

'And now,' Hyde said, 'I suggest you leave.'

'Not a chance,' I told the man, acting calmer than I felt. 'I have gone too far in this not to see the end.'

The man grew angry, but he couldn't wait... He drank the revolting potion in one gulp. I have never seen anything like it. His face twisted with pain. His eyes rolled to the limits of their sockets. With a blood-curdling scream, he collapsed to the floor, where he lay curled up and moaning."

"Finally he rose, careful to keep his back to me so I couldn't see his face. He seemed taller somehow, less agitated.

'Are you well?' I asked him.

Suddenly, he turned and barged past me for the door. But before he escaped into the night, I caught a glimpse of the man's face in the porch light. I... I..."

Lanyon scrunched his eyes shut, haunted by the memory.

"What did you see?" Utterson asked.

"What I saw, Utterson, was the face of Henry Jekyll!"

Chapter 8

The last night

Wind lashed at Utterson's face as he ran full pelt through the streets. Terrible thoughts raced through his mind. Could Lanyon's tale be true? Could Henry Jekyll and Edward Hyde really be the same person?

No! He refused to believe it. Surely Lanyon had lost his mind as well. But he had to find out. He reached Henry's house and hammered on the door.

Poole answered. A candle trembled in the butler's hand. His face was ghostly pale.

"Mr. Utterson," he gasped. "I am so glad you're here. I fear that my master has been murdered."

Tingling with fear, Utterson followed Poole into the house. He saw Jekyll's other servants cowering together by the fire. Something diabolical had indeed happened here. More than ever, Utterson was determined to get to the bottom of it.

Raising his shaky light, Poole led Utterson to Jekyll's laboratory. The door was locked, but Utterson heard someone moving inside.

"You saw Dr. Jekyll go into this room?" he asked Poole.

"As clear as day sir," the butler replied. "But soon after, I heard a piercing scream and the sound of smashing glass. Ever since, the door has been locked."

"Jekyll?" Utterson called, banging on the door. "I demand to see you."

"Go away," came the reply. "Please Utterson, just go away!"

Utterson felt a shiver of terror. That wasn't Jekyll's voice. It was Hyde.

"Stand back Poole," Utterson demanded. "I'll smash my way in."

Poole stepped back as the lawyer launched forward, smashing the laboratory door with his shoulder – once... twice... three times.

With each thunderous blow, the men heard another desperate cry from inside. "Please Utterson! Have mercy!"

The door crashed open and Utterson burst inside, his walking cane raised and ready to strike. But there was no need for the weapon.

Lying on the floor in a twisted heap, was the body of Edward Hyde. A bottle of red liquid rolled from the murderer's lifeless hand.

"Poison," Utterson said. "The fiend took his own life."

"Look sir," Poole said, examining a sheet of paper on the desk. "A note from Dr. Jekyll. It is addressed to you."

Utterson read the first line.

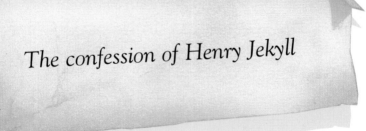

The confession of Henry Jekyll

Utterson stared at the corpse on the floor. Was Lanyon telling the truth? Could this man be his friend Henry too? The letter trembled in his hand as he began to read...

Chapter 9

The confession of Henry Jekyll

My dear Utterson,
Now that my life reaches its end, the
time has come to tell you everything about
Henry Jekyll and Edward Hyde.

Of me you already know much. I strived to
be a kind man and a good doctor. But more and
more I grew troubled by the violence I witnessed
in my work, the wounds from guns, knives, and
bloody battles.

I became convinced that all men were not truly one, but truly two – good and evil. I was determined to find a way to separate the two characters. At night I experimented with chemicals, creating a potion that I hoped would rid man of his capacity for evil.

One night, I drank it.

You have seen for yourself how the potion affected my body, Utterson, but you have not felt the indescribable pains. I felt a grinding in my bones, a sickness in my stomach. A terrible change came over me.

When I finally looked in a mirror, it wasn't Henry Jekyll that I saw, but a hideous, grinning stranger. This man told me his name was Edward Hyde.

I knew that Hyde was pure evil. So I quickly drank more of the potion, and again I became Henry Jekyll.

It should have ended there, but I became fascinated with my creation. I drank the potion regularly, and am ashamed to say that I welcomed the change.

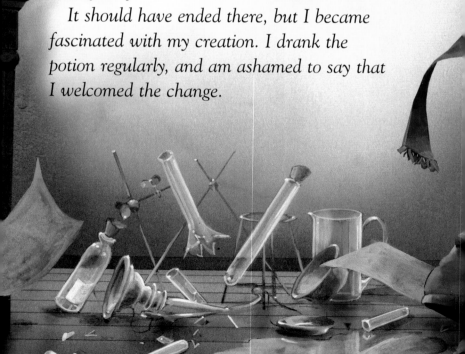

At night I stalked the streets as Edward Hyde. I felt alive, Utterson, I felt truly alive!

But gradually, Hyde began to take control of me. I began to change into him without even taking the potion. Fearing he would consume me completely, I had you write that will leaving everything I owned to Hyde. I even bought him his own house.

Hyde's evil grew worse and worse. He barged
into men, cursed at women, and trampled that
young girl in the street. I knew I should put an
end to him, but it was as if I was addicted to the
dark side of his nature.

Then, one night, Hyde went too far – and
murdered that poor man.

Suddenly all of London was hunting for Hyde. I began to take double and triple doses of the potion to stop myself from becoming him. I knew it might kill me, but I was desperate.

For three months, it succeeded. As you will remember Utterson, I became a new man. I was happy again. But it was not to last! One morning, as I walked in the park, I was wracked by the pains of the change. A moment later, I was Hyde again.

Hyde knew that he would be hanged if he was caught. So he turned to Lanyon to help secure the powder from my house. I am sure the doctor has told you what happened next, and that has led you now to my house.

But it is too late to save me. I have run out of the powder that stops me from becoming Edward Hyde. Soon Hyde will take control of me forever. But before that can happen, I am resolved to take my own life with poison.

I have created a monster, and now I must slay it. Yes, I feel him stirring inside me now...

Goodbye then Utterson. You were a true friend. Henry Jekyll.

"Sir?" Poole said.

Utterson flinched, crumpling the letter in his hands. He had been so lost in Jekyll's confession that he'd forgotten where he was.

He turned, gazing at the monster Edward Hyde lying dead on the floor.

This letter Utterson held would destroy Henry's reputation. He would be remembered as a monster. What had he once said?

"Help me Utterson, if not as my lawyer, then as my friend."

Utterson stepped to the fire and tossed Henry's confession onto the flames. Sparks crackled up the chimney, as shadows danced and darted around the laboratory walls.

"What about Dr. Jekyll sir?" Poole said.

"Henry Jekyll is gone Poole," Utterson said. "He will never be seen again."

Then the lawyer turned and walked out into the night.

Robert Louis Stevenson
(1850-1894)

Robert Louis Stevenson was born in Scotland in 1850. From a young age he suffered fevers brought on by the cold Scottish weather, so he spent much of his short life overseas. His travels inspired him to write plays, poems and popular adventure stories such as *Treasure Island* and *Kidnapped*. They made him one of the most famous writers of the 19th century. He died, aged 44, on a small island in the Pacific Ocean.

Usborne Quicklinks

For links to websites where you can find out more about Robert Louis Stevenson and his stories, go to the Usborne Quicklinks Website at **www.usborne-quicklinks.com** and enter the keyword 'stevenson'.

Please follow the internet safety guidelines displayed on the Usborne Quicklinks Website. Usborne Publishing is not responsible for the content of any website other than its own.

Debbie and Joey
in
God's World

by MORRIS and LENORE KIPPER

Illustrated by Audrey Komrad

SHENGOLD PUBLISHERS, INC.
New York

Library of Congress Catalog Card Number: 68-56183
Published by Shengold Publishers, Inc., New York
Text: Copyright © 1968 by Morris and Lenore Kipper
Illustrations: Copyright © by Audrey Komrad
All rights reserved
Printed in the United States of America

To Merle

Acknowledgments

To Dr. Sylvan D. Schwartzman, Professor of Jewish Religious Education at the Hebrew Union College—Jewish Institute of Religion, who gave us the inspiration for this book;

To the students of the Religious Schools of Temple Beth Sholom, Peabody, Mass., Temple Judea, Coral Gables, Fla., and Temple Beth Sholom, Miami Beach, Fla., who used the material in this book through the seven years of experimentation that yielded the finished work;

To Judy Kreutzer and Marcia Leventhal, dedicated teachers who developed a Teacher's Guide for this book;

To the many other primary grade teachers who checked the text for concept evaluation and vocabulary level;

To Doris Feder of Coral Gables, and Reene Kreincses of New York, for patiently typing and re-typing each improved edition;

To Gertrude Hirschler, Editor, for her unfailing cooperation and invaluable counsel;

To Moshe Sheinbaum, President of Shengold Publishers, whose excellent taste will never be equalled by a committee;

Our thanks go also to the Central Conference of American Rabbis for their kind permission to quote passages from the *Union Songster.*

And *aharon aharon haviv,* to all our friends and colleagues who gave us advice and encouragement throughout.

Dear Boys and Girls,

In another group of stories about **Debbie** and Joey you discovered many things about God's creations and God's power in the world. Their adventures have helped you understand a little bit about God's ways in the world. Now you can read more stories about Debbie and Joey. This time, you will see them discovering things about themselves.

In the Book of Genesis, the Bible tells the story of the Creation of the world. The story tells us that after a long time of creating the waters, the earth, the stars, the plants and the animals, God made man. But God made man different from His other creations. How are *you* different from God's other creations? What special gifts did God give you to make you different from other living things? In these stories you can join Debbie and Joey as they learn new things about God's wonderful creation, Man.

Rabbi Morris A. Kipper

THE STORY OF GENESIS

When God first made the world,
He made it full of light;
The sun to shine by day,
The moon and the stars by night.
And God saw that it was good.

He made it full of beauty;
Flowers and trees, fields and brooks.
And God saw that it was good.

He made it full of things to use;
Fruit and milk, iron and gold.
And God saw that it was good.

He made it full of living things;
Some that walk and some that fly,
Some that swim and some that creep.
And God saw that it was good.

To crown it all, the Lord made man;
With mind and heart, with hands and will,
To love and to think, to work and to play.

(Union Songster, p. 77)

And God saw everything that he had made,
And behold, it was very good.

(Genesis 1:31)

A MIRACLE AT DEBBIE'S HOUSE

"There are three partners in the forming of a human being: the father, the mother, and the Holy One, blessed be He."

(Talmud, Niddah 31a)

Have you ever asked yourself, "Where was I before I was born?" "How did I begin?" "How did I get born?" Debbie and Joey thought about these things. Many boys and girls think about these questions, but sometimes they don't ask them out loud. They keep on thinking about them without finding any answers.

You had a beginning. So did your parents and everyone else you know. This beginning is part of the story of how all living things keep on coming into the world.

A MIRACLE AT DEBBIE'S HOUSE

One night Debbie was awakened in the middle of the night. Something wonderful was going to happen in her family.

"Debbie," Mrs. Berman whispered softly. But Debbie did not move. Her mother sat down on the bed and took her hand. "Debbie, it's mother." But still she didn't wake. Mrs. Berman put the light on. Slowly Debbie opened her eyes.

"What is it?" She rubbed her sleepy eyes. "Is it time for school?" she asked. She lifted the shade. It was still dark outside. It must be in the middle of the night she thought. "What's wrong, Mommy?"

Mother put her arm around her. "Nothing, dear. I just woke you to tell you something very important. Daddy has to take me to the hospital now. Do you remember I told you when it was time for our new baby to be born I would have to go to the hospital. It's time for me to go now. There the nurses and doctors will be able to help me have the new baby. Grandma's here. She'll give you breakfast and help you get ready for school while I am at the hospital. I'll be back home in a few days. Meanwhile, I'll call you every day, for sure."

"Why can't I come to the hospital with you and wait with Daddy? I won't bother anyone! Please?" Debbie begged.

"Don't you remember that children aren't allowed to visit in the hospital? Besides, in the morning you'll want to tell your friends at school. Daddy will tell you as soon as the baby is born." Mrs. Berman turned out the light and tucked Debbie's blankets in. "I love you and I'll miss you, Debbie. Try and help Grandma all you can while I'm away." She kissed Debbie on her forehead.

Debbie hugged Mother. "Does it hurt to have a baby?" she whispered.

"Just a little," her mother answered, "but I won't mind because I'll be thinking that soon there will be a little brother or a little sister for you and me to care for and to love. Better get some sleep now. We'll talk some more when I come home."

Debbie tried to fall asleep again. But she kept thinking about the new baby. Would it be a sister or brother? Would it cry a lot? Would she have to share her toys? Before she knew it, it was morning and she could smell waffles cooking in the kitchen. She could hear Grandma and Daddy talking. So Daddy was back from the hospital!

"Lisa? What a fine name," she heard Grandma say. "Very pretty."

Debbie thought a minute. Then she came running into the kitchen. "Lisa! It's a baby girl! I have a sister! Daddy, is it true, do I have a baby sister?"

Dr. Berman lifted Debbie in his arms and hugged her very tightly. "You guessed it, sweetheart. Your little sister was born just an hour ago. Mommy's feeling fine and sends you a big kiss."

"When can I see her? Can we go to the hospital? What does the baby look like? What does she do? Can she talk? What does she eat? Can I bring her some cookies?"

Grandma smiled. "My goodness! Wait a minute, young lady! Hold the questions. Look at the time! Hurry, get washed and dressed! Daddy'll tell you everything while you have your breakfast."

"Aw Grandma, do I have to go to school today?"

"Can't we make this a holiday? After all, it's my sister Lisa's birthday. Get it Dad? *Birth Day?*" They all laughed.

When Debbie sat down for breakfast she started asking questions all over again. "What does she look like, Dad?"

"Well," her father answered, "she looks a little like your mother, a little like you, and even a little like me."

Debbie giggled. "Like you? Now how could my sister look like a man?"

"You know that fathers help make babies, too," her father said. "In fact, it takes three to make a baby. It takes a very tiny egg in Mommy's body, and an even tinier *cell* from Daddy's body. When the two of them, the egg and the cell, get together God helps a little baby start growing inside Mommy."

"And with the help of God," Grandma added, "the baby grows hands, feet, eyes and everything it needs before it is ready to be born into this world. *This is the wonderful way in which God creates a new life.*"

"God willing," Dr. Berman said, "our new baby will grow up to be a fine little girl, just like you, Debbie."

"Gosh, Dad, was I born the same way?" Debbie asked.

"Yes," her father replied. "A part of me and a part of Mommy were put together with God's help and here you are. You and Lisa each have something of Mommy and some of Daddy, but you two won't be exactly alike. God gives us all life, but we are made to be a little different from each other, even when we are sisters and brothers.

"Are you finished?" Grandma asked. "The school bus will be here very soon."

Debbie gobbled down the last bite of waffle, drank her milk, kissed her father goodbye and ran to call for Joey, next door. Joey was just coming out of his house.

"Joey, Joey," she called. "Hurry up. Guess what? I'm a sister. I mean, I have a baby sister! And, you know what, part of me is like my Daddy, and part of me is like my Mommy, and part of me is like God. Isn't that wonderful? *I'm a little like God.*"

"Okay, okay, so you're a sister. But what's this about being God?"

Debbie didn't answer right away. She was still thinking about what her father had told her.

Suddenly she shouted, "Joey, I'm not God, *I'm a miracle. And so are you. No one else can be exactly like us, not even sisters or brothers. God made us each to be special.*"

The two children saw the school bus coming down the street. They ran to the corner to meet the other children.

"Hurry Joey, Hurry, Debbie!" the children called.

"Whew, just made it, didn't we?" panted Joey. "Hey kids, Debbie has a new baby sister."

"That's great," said one girl.

"Oh boy, now you'll have to share everything," said another friend.

"It'll be fun, Debbie, to have someone to play with all the time," added another.

The bus stopped at the corner. As the children got on, they told the good news about Debbie's new sister to their friend, Mr. Jones, the bus driver.

That night when Debbie was in bed with her favorite doll, she couldn't fall asleep. She was so excited. She wondered about the new baby. She missed her mother's goodnight kiss. As she hugged her doll she knew that soon she would be able to hold a real baby. In her prayers that night, she gave thanks to God for the new miracle of life—her sister, Lisa.

"Hello," he said. Then he asked, "Mrs. Berman, is there anything wrong with Lisa? Debbie said she can't do anything but sleep and cry."

Mrs. Berman smiled. She walked toward the bedroom. "Come in here. I'll show you some of the tricks Lisa has learned already. Of course, it isn't the kind of tricks you and Debbie do on the climbing bars."

"Joey, can you play baseball very well?" Debbie's mother asked.

"Not too well," Joey answered, "but I'm learning. My dad and I practice whenever we can."

"How long have you been practicing with your father?" Mrs. Berman asked.

"Gosh, I can't remember. I think we started playing catch when I was in first grade."

"And you can't play baseball yet?" asked Debbie.

"Can you?" answered Joey.

"Gee, I guess she's not too smart," said Joey.

Mrs. Berman heard the children talking. "Hello, Joey. It's nice to see you, again."

"Wah, Wah, Wah." There went Baby Lisa, again. Finally, Mrs. Berman, Debbie's mother, came out, picked up Lisa, and took her inside.

Why does Lisa cry so much? Joey wondered. Was she sick? Did something hurt her? He climbed down the bars and went indoors.

"Mom," he called. "When can I go to Debbie's house? Can't you call Mrs. Berman and ask her if I can come over?"

"Well, all right," Mrs. Gordon replied, "but if she says yes you must be sure to do just what she tells you when you are there."

"Okay, Mom, okay. But please call her."

Joey was very excited when Mrs. Berman said yes. He ran next door.

"Oh, hi Joey," Debbie said as she opened the door to let him in.

"Hi Debbie. I came over to see your new baby. Your Mom says it's all right for me to come now."

"Come in," Debbie answered. "You don't want to see the new baby, Joey. Let's play instead."

"Why not?" asked Joey.

"All she does is sleep and sleep, and cry and cry. She can't even see me yet. She doesn't even smile when I talk to her."

LEARNING TRICKS

"Then the Lord God formed man . . ., and man became a living soul."   *(Gen.2:7)*

The story of the creation of the world tells us that man became a *living soul*. The Rabbis tell us this means that at the time we are born God gave us the power to think and learn and understand.

Can you remember the time when you were a baby? Do you think you were able to think and learn when you were that small? Debbie's new baby sister Lisa has come home from the hospital. But Joey hasn't been able to see the baby yet. When he does, he finds out some surprising things about babies.

LEARNING TRICKS

One day after school, Joey was climbing on his climbing bars. He liked to do many tricks on them. He liked to put boards on the top bars and sit all the way up there. Sometimes Debbie would join him and they would bring up sandwiches and pretend they were in an airplane flying high above the ground. But lately Debbie hadn't been coming over to play very often. Joey thought that she was too busy playing with her new baby sister. Joey looked over at Debbie's porch. He saw the baby carriage, covered with a net. Suddenly, he heard crying.

"Wah, Wah, Wah . . ."

"Wow, what a lot of noise! I wonder what's wrong?" he thought. He wanted very much to see the new baby, but his mother wouldn't let him visit Debbie's house yet. The baby had only been home a week. He wanted to see the baby. He was the youngest in his family, so he had not been around babies very often.

"Girls aren't supposed to know how to play baseball. But if I were a boy, I bet I could even play basketball if I practiced!"

"Is that so!" Joey shouted.

"Wah, Wah, Wah . . ." Lisa was crying again.

"I don't think Lisa likes the sound of your shouting, Joey," said Mrs. Berman.

"I'm sorry," Joey whispered.

"Me too," added Debbie.

"That's all right," Mrs. Berman said. "I thought you two came in to see Lisa's tricks. I just asked you how long it took you to learn how to play baseball, Joey, because Lisa has learned to do some tricks already and she is only two weeks old. Watch closely now."

Mrs. Berman picked the baby up carefully. She took a bottle of water and put it to Lisa's lips. Lisa opened her mouth and began drinking as fast as she could.

"Gosh, look at her go!" Joey exclaimed. "She knows just what to do with that bottle. Who taught her to drink?"

"No one really taught her," Debbie's mother answered. "She seemed to know the minute she was born. And she knows other things too."

"What else?" asked Joey.

"She knows how to ask for milk when she is hungry. She knows how to tell us when she needs a clean diaper."

"Mother, I've never heard Lisa ask for anything," Debbie said. "Why, she doesn't even talk."

Mrs. Berman smiled, "Oh she doesn't talk with words. Somehow she seems to know that if she is hungry or if she is unhappy all she has to do is . . ."

"Cry!" Debbie answered.

"How did she learn that?" asked Joey.

"Did you teach her while she was still inside you?" Debbie asked.

Her mother laughed. "No, not I. Do you remember who is our partner in creating babies?"

"It takes a mother and a father and God to make a new baby," Debbie answered.

"Right you are, Debbie," Mrs. Berman said. "God makes it possible for babies to know and do certain things from the minute they are born. Each month that Lisa grows older, God makes it possible for her to learn how to do more things."

Mrs. Berman put Lisa back into the crib. Joey looked at her again. Her hands were so tiny next to his. Debbie and Joey followed Mrs. Berman out of the bedroom and to the kitchen for cookies and milk.

"Did God teach you how to be a good mother and Daddy how to be a good doctor?" Debbie asked her mother.

"Partly," Mrs. Berman answered. "I guess God had a lot to do with your father becoming a good doctor. God gave Daddy a good brain so that he could learn all the things a doctor must know in school; but God also helped him learn how to love people and really care about them."

Joey looked puzzled. "When my teacher in school teaches me spelling I know she is teaching me. But how do I know when God is teaching me?"

"God is always teaching us things," Debbie's mother said. "Remember a part of you is like God. But you must learn to know the times when God is teaching you. We don't hear God teaching and speaking to us with our ears, like you hear your teacher, Joey. But we can learn to know what God teaches us through the way we feel and the way we think. Just as great men like Abraham and Moses learned to know the teachings of God."

When the children had finished their cookies and milk they went outdoors to play.

"Come on, Debbie," Joey called. "With the brain God gave me I can teach you some *new tricks* on the climbing bars!"

A PARTY FOR LISA

"Each child brings his own blessing into the world."
(Yiddish proverb)

Do you remember the story of Abraham, the first Jew, and his wife Sarah? They were married for many years but did not have any children. Then, when they were both very old, something wonderful happened. They had a little boy whom they named Isaac, which means to laugh or be happy. Isaac did make them very happy.

Mothers and fathers are very happy when they have children. They want to give thanks to God for this gift of a new life. In this story, Debbie and Joey find out the special way in which Debbie's parents gave thanks to God for the new baby, Lisa.

A PARTY FOR LISA

"Hurry up, Mom, we'll be late!" Joey and his family were getting ready to go to Sabbath Services. It was a special night. Every month, Joey went to the Synagogue for Family Services. He liked to hear the children's choir sing. Some of his friends were in it. It was fun to see the children from his Religious School class all dressed up. And afterwards, there always were delicious cookies and punch for everyone. Sometimes, there was a birthday cake, too. Tonight was even more special. Tonight, Debbie's family would have a Baby-Naming Ceremony. Joey didn't know exactly what that was, but he was happy to go. It would be like a party for the new baby. Lisa was now a month old.

Joey and his mother and father came into the sanctuary. He saw Debbie and her family sitting in front. Soon the service began. Joey always felt very good when he sat next to his parents in the synagogue.

He liked to sing along with the choir and the Rabbi. After a while, the Rabbi asked Dr. and Mrs. Berman to come forward. He asked them to stand in front of the Ark, where the Torah Scrolls were kept.

Then he heard the Rabbi say:

"Our God, Creator of all life, we thank you for the special gift of a new life. Happy parents have come to this sanctuary to find Your help as they begin the holy task of raising this child. We give this child the name of Lisa, to be known in Hebrew as "Eleesheva." May she grow in body and mind to be a blessing to her parents through her good deeds."

Then Dr. and Mrs. Berman read a prayer together:

"Our God, we are very grateful for the wonderful gift of a new life. Teach us to be good parents."

Soon, services were over. Joey turned to his father and said, "I know we have prayers to give thanks to God for our bread and food, but who ever heard of giving thanks to God for girls?"

Mr. Gordon laughed. "Well, what's wrong with that? We even thank God for little boys!"

"Oh, yeah? Did you say a prayer for me when I was born?"

"We certainly did," Mr. Gordon answered.

"But you said that when I was a baby. I'll bet you're sorry you ever said thank you to God for me, now that I'm not a baby anymore!"

"That's not true," Mr. Gordon said. "In fact, your Mother and I thank God every day for giving us such a wonderful boy. God gives children to parents to make them happy and most of the time boys and girls do make their parents very happy and proud."

Debbie and her family passed Joey's row as they left the sanctuary. "Come on, Joey," she called. "You should see all the good things there are to eat!"

Joey joined Debbie. Together, they went straight to the table where punch and cookies were being served. There were brownies and cupcakes, peanuts and candy. Joey could hardly wait! He took a little of everything.

"This is a great party!" Joey said.

"Yes, I guess so," Debbie answered. "Mom and Dad are really happy with Lisa. And boy, the presents she gets from everybody! Whenever anyone comes over, all they want to do is see the baby. Nobody cares about me anymore."

Joey thought he saw tears in Debbie's eyes. He tried to make her feel better. "Don't worry, Debbie," he said, "they love you even if you aren't a baby any-more. My Dad told me that." He thought a minute. "But what I don't get is how they can still love us when they are yelling at us!"

"Parents sure are hard to understand," Debbie said.

Debbie's father came over to their table. "Hi, how's my big girl?"

"Fine, I guess," Debbie answered.

But Dr. Berman knew that something was troubling her. He bent down and whispered, "Why don't we go to the park tomorrow afternoon? Just you, Mommy and me."

Debbie was surprised. "Really, just the three of us? What about Lisa?"

"Don't worry. Mommy'll get a sitter for her. She is only a baby and can't have much fun at the park yet. When she is older, like you are, she will be able to come with us more often."

"Okay, Dad, that'll be fun." Joey and Debbie looked at each other with a little smile.

Dr. Berman went off to talk with a friend.

"See, didn't I tell you?" bragged Joey. "They still care about you. Even though there's a new baby in the house. Let's go get some more cookies and punch. Say, too bad your sister Lisa can't even be at her own party!"

Debbie laughed. She was feeling better now. They went back to the table. Joey started filling his plate again with brownies.

"Hey, come on, take some more," Joey said to Debbie.

"No, thank you," Debbie answered. "I don't want to have a stomach ache tomorrow, especially not tomorrow. Tomorrow will be a wonderful day for me."

THE WONDERFUL MACHINE

"To crown it all, the Lord made man;
With mind and heart, with hands and will,
To love and to think, to work and to play."
(Union Songster, p. 77)

When God created you, He created a wonderful thing. Do you remember when you couldn't ride a bicycle, or stand on roller skates or catch a ball? Baby Lisa can't do any of these things yet. This year, you will be able to do things you couldn't do so very well last year. Or maybe you'll be able to understand some things better now than you could before. In this story, just as Joey was getting good at playing football, he ran into some unexpected trouble.

THE WONDERFUL MACHINE

Debbie and Joey liked to get to Religious School a little early Sunday morning. This gave them a chance to play and talk with their friends before class. This morning Joey was in a special hurry to get there. He had just gotten a football for his birthday. He brought it to show to his friends. As they got out of the car, Joey called to his friends, "Hey, you guys, come here!"

Some of the boys hurried over. "Wow, what a neat football!" one of them shouted.

"And look, it's official size, too!" another friend exclaimed. "Let me see it, Joey, will you? Pass it over here," said one of the older boys.

The boys had a great time passing, kicking, blocking and dashing across the playground. Debbie watched them for a while. "Hurry!" she cried out as she saw Joey catch a pass and run. She was about to go inside, when she saw the boys huddled together. Then she saw the game had stopped. She hadn't heard the bell yet.

"I bet they're having an argument," she thought.
Suddenly, one of the boys came running across the
field.

"Where's the teacher? Where is she? Joey's hurt!"
Quickly, Debbie, some other girls and their teacher,
Mrs. Jacobs, rushed over to Joey.

"Oooh, ohhh," Debbie heard Joey moan. They saw him sitting on the ground, bent over, holding his right hand in his lap.

"What happened?" Mrs. Jacobs asked.

All the boys tried to tell her at the same time.

"One at a time, please!"

Joey had hurt his hand when he was being tackled. Mrs. Jacobs helped him to the office and called his parents.

"Oh, dear, there's the bell! I have to go inside." Mrs. Jacobs turned to Joey.

Joey was sitting there, holding back the tears, trying not to show how much his hand hurt him.

"Debbie," Mrs. Jacobs said, "stay here with Joey until his parents come. I'm sure they will want to take him to the doctor."

Soon Mr. and Mrs. Gordon were there and took Joey to the hospital. Debbie went with them. As soon as they got to the hospital, the nurse took Joey into a special room. Mr. and Mrs. Gordon and Debbie sat down and waited in the doctor's office.

"Gee, Mrs. Gordon, I never saw Joey cry like this before," Debbie said. "His hand must really hurt. Why does his hand look so different?"

"I'm afraid his hand is broken," Mrs. Gordon said.

"Broken?" said Debbie. "But it isn't bleeding or anything!"

"You can't see it because the bones are covered by the skin," Mrs. Gordon said.

Just then, Joey came out. He wasn't crying any more. In fact, he was smiling. His right arm and wrist were covered by a big white plaster cast. "Look at this!" he shouted. "I needed a cast for my broken hand. Now all my friends can put their names on it. Would you like to be first, Debbie?"

Debbie was puzzled. Before, Joey had been in great pain. He had even been crying. Now, here he was, smiling and happy about his cast. "No, thank you," she answered. "Why don't *you* be the first to put your own name on your own cast?"

"Good idea! Give me a pen, and I will sign my name." Debbie handed him her pen, but Joey just stood there, staring at everybody.

"I . . . I can't." The tears were about to start again. "I can't write." Joey looked at his mother. "Mom, I can't write, and . . . and, I won't be able to eat, or get dressed. I won't be able to do anything!"

Just then the doctor came out. "Well, young man, I hope at least you made a touchdown getting this broken hand."

"Hello, Doctor," Mr. Gordon said. "Thanks for hurrying over. How long will Joey need this cast?"

"That depends on how fast he heals it."

"How *I* heal it?" Joey asked. "Doctor, aren't you the one who's supposed to fix my hand?"

The doctor and Mr. Gordon smiled at each other. "In a way, Joey, I can help your hand get better, but it's *really you, yourself,* that heals your own hand. God has made our bodies in such a wonderful way that with a little help from doctors our bodies can repair themselves whenever there is a broken bone."

"Oh, I get it!" said Joey. "Like when Dad takes the car to the garage to get a part fixed by the mechanic."

The doctor and Mr. Gordon laughed. "You've got an idea there, Joey," his Dad said, "and in a way you're right. The human body is like a machine in many ways. Each part of the body has a special job to do, and when all these parts work together, they keep us alive and happy. Just like the parts of a car work together to make it run."

The nurse came in with the X-ray pictures of Joey's hand.

The doctor held the picture to the light.

"Wow, look at my hand!" Joey exclaimed.

"But where's the skin on that picture?" asked Debbie.

"Debbie, you don't know anything! Don't you know an X-ray only takes the picture of what's inside your hand under the skin?"

"Oh," Debbie said shyly. "It's like magic. The skin disappears."

"Exactly," said the doctor. "That is how we could see the place where Joey's hand was broken." He pointed to the bone on the X-ray.

"Gee, I always thought my hand was just one big bone, but look at all these!" Joey began to count the bones he saw in the X-ray.

"There are twenty-seven bones in your right hand, Joey," the doctor told him.

"In mine, too?" Debbie asked.

"In yours, too," the doctor said, smiling. In your hand, in my hand, in every human hand there are twenty-seven small bones. But still — each person's hand is different from anyone's else's."

"I know," said Joey, "our fingerprints show that!"

"No one else in the whole world can have the same fingerprints as you," the doctor said.

The doctor put Joey's X-ray picture into his file. "Now I want to see you again in two weeks. And, if you're careful and don't have any more accidents, your hand should be able to heal itself in about four weeks."

"Four weeks!" exclaimed Joey. At first, he didn't like the idea of not being able to use his hand for that long.

"Don't feel bad, Joey," said Debbie. "Just think, you won't have to do any written work in school."

As they were leaving the office, they passed a big, white cabinet with large glass doors. On the shelves were many kinds of shining tools. Joey looked in. "Wow, you have more tools than my Dad has in his tool chest."

The doctor walked over to the cabinet. "For every little job I need a different tool to help people get better." He opened the door. "This one is for holding something in place."

"Like my Dad's vise?" asked Joey.

"Yes. And here's one for pounding and one for squeezing."

"Doctor?" said Debbie. "The tools you need to help people are wonderful, but you know what? My hands can do all that those tools can do and more!"

"Smart girl!" The doctor patted Debbie's head. "Our hands are wonderful little machines. They can hold or grasp things, open and close, shake, press, pound, scrape, squeeze and a lot more. All my tools are no good to me as a doctor unless I can use them with the hands God created."

"Gosh, God is a Super Creator," said Debbie. "God gave me two hands that can do as many things as the tools or machines that are made in a factory."

"And they don't even need oiling or sharpening," laughed Joey.

"But they do need washing!" Mr. Gordon said.

All the way home, Debbie and Joey talked about how he would get along without the use of his right hand. They had never realized before, how important their hands were to them.

A NEW FRIEND

"The Lord helps the blind to see."

(Psalms 146:8)*

Do you remember the stories about Moses? He became a great leader of the Jewish People many years ago. Moses led the Jewish People out of Egypt when they were slaves to the King. But did you know he was once afraid to go to the King to ask him to let the people go? Why? Moses could not speak well. He was afraid the King would not listen to him. Even so, Moses became a great Jewish leader. God helps men to overcome their handicaps. God tells us, "to be strong and of good courage."

Joey was afraid he wouldn't be able to do anything with his hand in a cast. It made him very sad. But, little by little, Joey learned to get along even though he couldn't use his right hand. He had to find new ways to do things. In this story, Debbie and Joey meet a new friend. This new friend is different from them in one way. He has had to learn to find new ways to do many things. His name is David.

---

* Free translation of "The Lord openeth the eyes of the blind."
  (Psalms 146:8)

A NEW FRIEND

Some weeks had passed since Joey had broken his hand. During that time, he had learned to do many things with his left hand that he never thought he'd be able to do. He had gotten used to the cast.

One day Debbie and Joey had just come home from school when they saw a moving van down the street.

"Look, new neighbors are moving into that house!" exclaimed Joey. "Let's go see who it is, and if they have any kids."

The two of them ran down the street. They watched the moving men bring in the furniture, piece by piece. They watched to see if there were any children's things on the truck. They didn't see any bikes. The next thing to come out was a big piano. But they didn't see anything that might tell them that there would be children moving in. Debbie and Joey walked back to Debbie's house for some cookies and milk.

The next day, after school, Debbie and Joey were playing outdoors. They saw a car at the house where the moving van had been the day before. A man and a woman got out—and a little boy. He looked about Joey's size.

"Terrific!" shouted Joey. "Come on, Debbie, let's go meet them."

"Don't you think we should wait?" Debbie asked.

"Naw, I'll bet that kid will be happy to know there are other kids around here."

Before the new family could get inside, Debbie and Joey were standing there, introducing themselves.

"Hi, I'm Joey Gordon, and this is Debbie Berman. We live down there at the end of the block. Are you the new neighbors?" Joey was talking so fast he hardly gave them a chance to answer. "What's your name? What grade are you in? Where did you come from?"

The mother and father looked at one another and smiled. "Hello," said the mother. "Yes, we are your new neighbors. I'm Mrs. Brown and this is our son David."

"Hi," said David. "We're from Chicago."

Debbie looked at David. Something seemed a little different about him. But she didn't say anything. Mr. Brown invited the children into the house. As they were going in, Debbie and Joey noticed that Mr. Brown was helping David up the steps.

"I wonder if he had a broken leg, like I have a broken hand," Joey whispered to Debbie.

After they were inside, Mrs. Brown said, "You are always welcome to visit us and to play with David and his toys and games. But first there is something you must know."

She'll probably tell us about taking care of toys and picking things up, like Mom always tells me at home, Debbie thought.

"David is a very special boy," Mrs. Brown went on. David sees with his hands. He cannot see with his eyes, so God has helped him learn to see with his hands."

"You mean he's blind?" Joey asked. He had never met a blind person before.

"That's right," answered David. "But I can still play many games and I can see many things with my hands."

Debbie came closer to David. "Gosh, can you see my face with your hands?"

David put his fingers over Debbie's face. Slowly, he touched her eyes, then her nose, her mouth and her cheeks. Then he felt her hair. "I think you are a pretty girl, Debbie. I hope we'll be good friends.

Debbie blushed and giggled.

"That's neat," added Joey, "What else can you *see* with your hands?"

"I can read books, I can add numbers, and a lot of other things," answered David.

"But, how could you read my books, if you can't see the words?" Debbie asked.

"David can't read *your* books, but he can read *his* books," Mr. Brown said. "Here, David, show them how you can read with your hands."

David's parents went out to the car to get some of their suitcases.

David opened the book his father had given him and began to read aloud. Joey looked over David's shoulder, at the page in the book. He could not see any words or letters. "Aw, I know that trick. You're just pretending. Why, there are no words on that page!"

Debbie came over to look. "All I see are little bumps all over the page. They look like goose-pimples."

David laughed. "I guess they do look like goose bumps, but that is how I read. I feel the little bumps with my fingers. Each group of bumps is a word to me. It's called Braille writing."

"Braille?" asked Joey. He had never heard the word before. "Gosh, its like a code, isn't it? Boy, would I like to know how to do that."

"Would you really like to learn?" asked David.

"I sure would. Would you teach us? Would you?"

Mr. and Mrs. Brown came in with the suitcases.

Joey and Debbie asked if they could help.

"David's going to teach us how to read with our hands." Debbie said.

"That's wonderful," said David's mother. "But, first, David must learn to know his new home. He must study it carefully. Then he'll have time to teach you Braille."

"Study a house?" Debbie asked.

"Yes. David must learn where every piece of furniture is. He must learn where every door is. He must remember where every thing is in his new home."

"I have an idea," said Debbie. "Joey and I will teach David all about his new house, a little every day after school, and he can teach us how to read Braille."

"It's a deal," said David. "Let's start right now."

Debbie and Joey led David to each piece of furniture in the living room.

After a short time, David said, "Now let me try it alone. Over here is the couch, and this is the table in front of it." He moved to the corner. "And here is the television set." Then he moved to the other side of the room. "Here is my piano." He sat down on the bench and began to play.

Debbie and Joey were very surprised to hear him play the piano so well.

"Gosh, you better not play in front of my Mom," Joey said. "She'll make me practice even more."

Debbie looked at her watch. It was nearly five o'clock. "Oh, oh, I forgot to call my Mom and tell her where I went. May I use your phone, David?"

"Sure, and if you lead me to it, I'll dial the number for you."

As Debbie said each number, David dialed cor-‑rectly. Joey watched with great surprise. "How can you dial a telephone number when you can't see the numbers?"

Mr. Brown heard Joey's question. "I think you can see now how David can see with his hands. Because David cannot use his eyes to see with, he has learned to live and learn and play by using the other wonderful parts of his body. David has a very good memory. He can remember where things are better than you and I can."

"Whenever we are not able to use one part of our bodies, God helps us to learn new ways to get along."

"That's what happened to me when I broke my hand," said Joey. I was scared when I wasn't able to do anything with my hand. I thought I wouldn't be able to do anything or have any fun. But in a short time I even learned to eat with my other hand!"

"Good for you," said Mr. Brown. "That's the way David has learned to see. Because he cannot use his eyes, God has helped him learn to see with his hands, his ears and his memory. David has found new ways to go on living, learning and playing."

"TEMPLE ISRAEL"

"Debbie," called David, "your Mom is on the phone. Don't you want to talk to her?"

"Oh, I almost forgot!" Debbie took the phone from David and told her mother she'd be right home. "Come on, Joey. We have to leave now. Bye, David, we'll come over after school tomorrow."

"I really want to find out about this Braille thing," added Joey.

"I'll be waiting for you," said David. David found his way to the piano and started to play. He felt very happy. Debbie and Joey were going to be his new friends.

"To crown it all, the Lord made man;
With mind and heart, with hands and will,
To love and to think, to work and to play."